For Ivan Matthew Geras Jones – A.G.
For my lovely sister, Dilly – S.W.

First published in Great Britain in 2012 by
Piccadilly Press Ltd, 5 Castle Road, London NW1 8PR
www.piccadillypress.co.uk

Designed by Simon Davis
Printed and bound in China by WKT
Colour reproduction by Dot Gradations

ISBN: 978 1 84812 251 2 (h/b)
ISBN: 978 1 84812 250 5 (p/b)

1 3 5 7 9 10 8 6 4 2

It's Time for Bed

By Adèle Geras
Illustrated by Sophy Williams

Piccadilly Press • London

"It's time for bed now," said Mother Hare.

"*But I don't feel sleepy . . .*" said Little Hare,

". . . and I think Mouse should go to bed first."

"I'll sing him a mouse's lullaby.

You've scurried about
among the leaves,
among the leaves that the trees have shed.
Come home, little mouse
to your little mouse house.
Sleep through the night
in your little mouse bed."

"*Is Mouse asleep now?*"

"Yes, he is."

"But Bird's not in bed, so I can't go to sleep.
Is there a lullaby for a bird?"

"There is and I'll sing it to you.

Bird on the branch,
you've sung your song.
Tuck your feathered head
under one soft wing
and sleep and sleep
the whole night long.
Tomorrow there'll be
another song:
another song
you want to sing."

"Is Bird asleep?"

"Yes, he is. And it's bath time now."

"But I don't want a bath yet. Froggy's still awake.
Can you sing him a lullaby for frogs?"

"Yes, and then you must get into the water.

How about a lily pad?
How about a log?
What's the best bed
for a very sleepy frog?
Here's a croaky lullaby:
sleep well, Frog.
Not on a lily pad,
not on a log,
but under a blanket
of grass and reeds.
That's what a
sleepy
Froggy
needs."

"I think he's gone to sleep now, hasn't he?"

"He has. He's fast asleep, so get into the water.
The ducks like splashing about as well.

Now you've had your bath,
so let's put the ducks on a branch for the night."

"*But first can they have a lullaby?*"

"Quack and splash
and splash and quack.
We've had a good time in the stream with you.
We'll see you tomorrow when you come back."

"Bunny isn't asleep yet. I think she wants a lullaby, too. Can she have the one that Granny always sings to me?"

"Yes, I like that lullaby too.

Hush-a-bye Bunny
in your pretty cradle,
wrapped in a blanket
as warm as warm.
Nothing will hurt you
while you are sleeping;
while I am keeping you
safe from harm.

Bunny's asleep now.
It's time for bed."

*"I feel sleepy now, but Little Bear hasn't had a lullaby yet.
I know he'd like one."*

"You went on a little bears' picnic today,
down in the woods with your little bear friends.
There was chocolate ice cream and buns and sweets.
And when you're in bed and fast asleep
you'll have ice cream all over again
in happy ice cream-eating dreams."

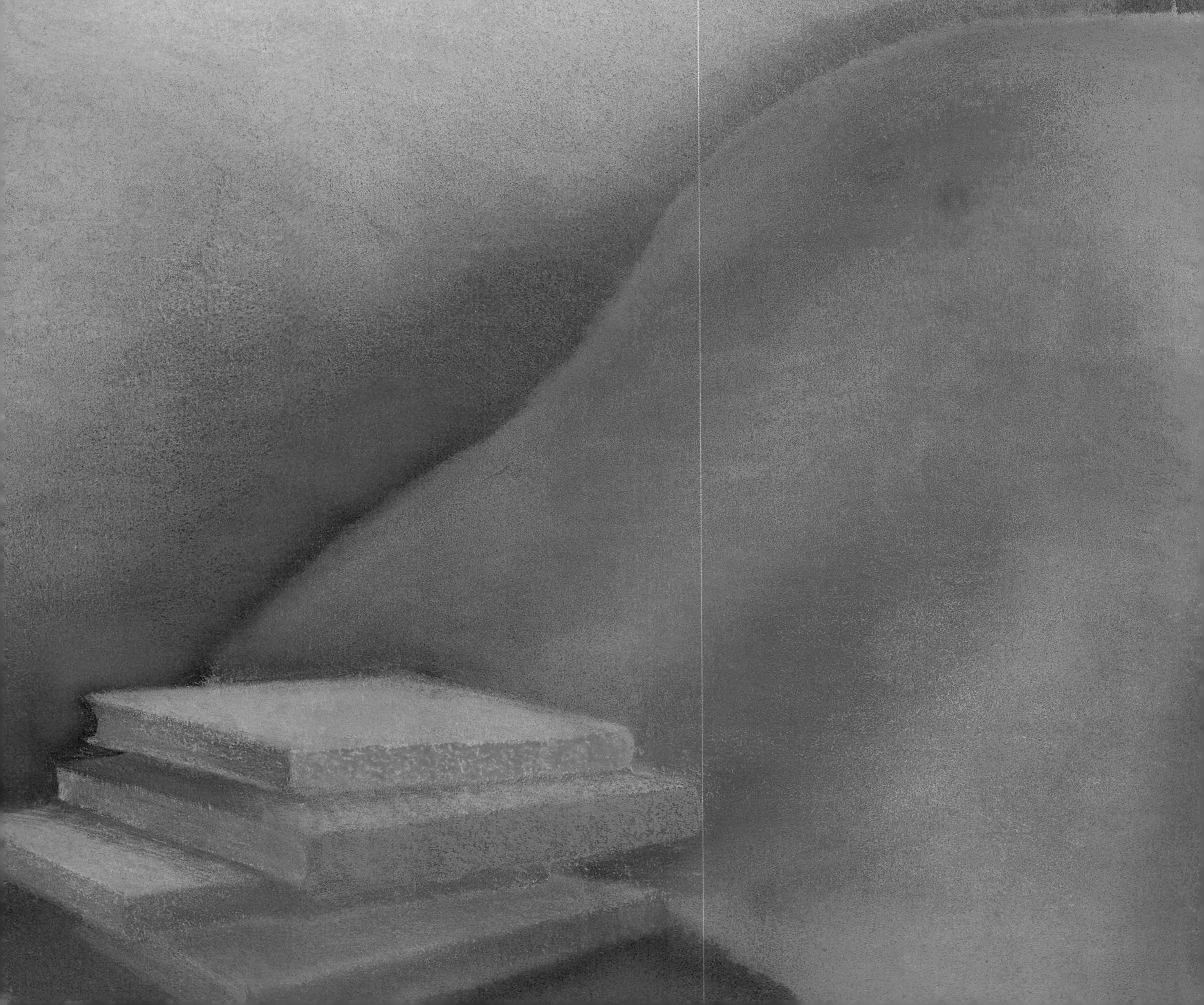

"*Is Little Bear sleeping?*"

"Yes, he is. He's snoozing away.
Do you feel sleepy now?"

"*I think so, but I'm very thirsty. Can I have a drink, please?*"

"Yes, here's a drink. And now I'm going to give you a cuddle and kiss you goodnight.

The very last lullaby is for you.

Everything round you
is fast asleep.
Mouse is dreaming
and Bird is too.
Little Bear is asleep,
Bunny's safe in her bed;
the sun's gone down
as you can see.
Frog is snoring,
snuffly snores
and the ducks are asleep
on the branch of a tree.

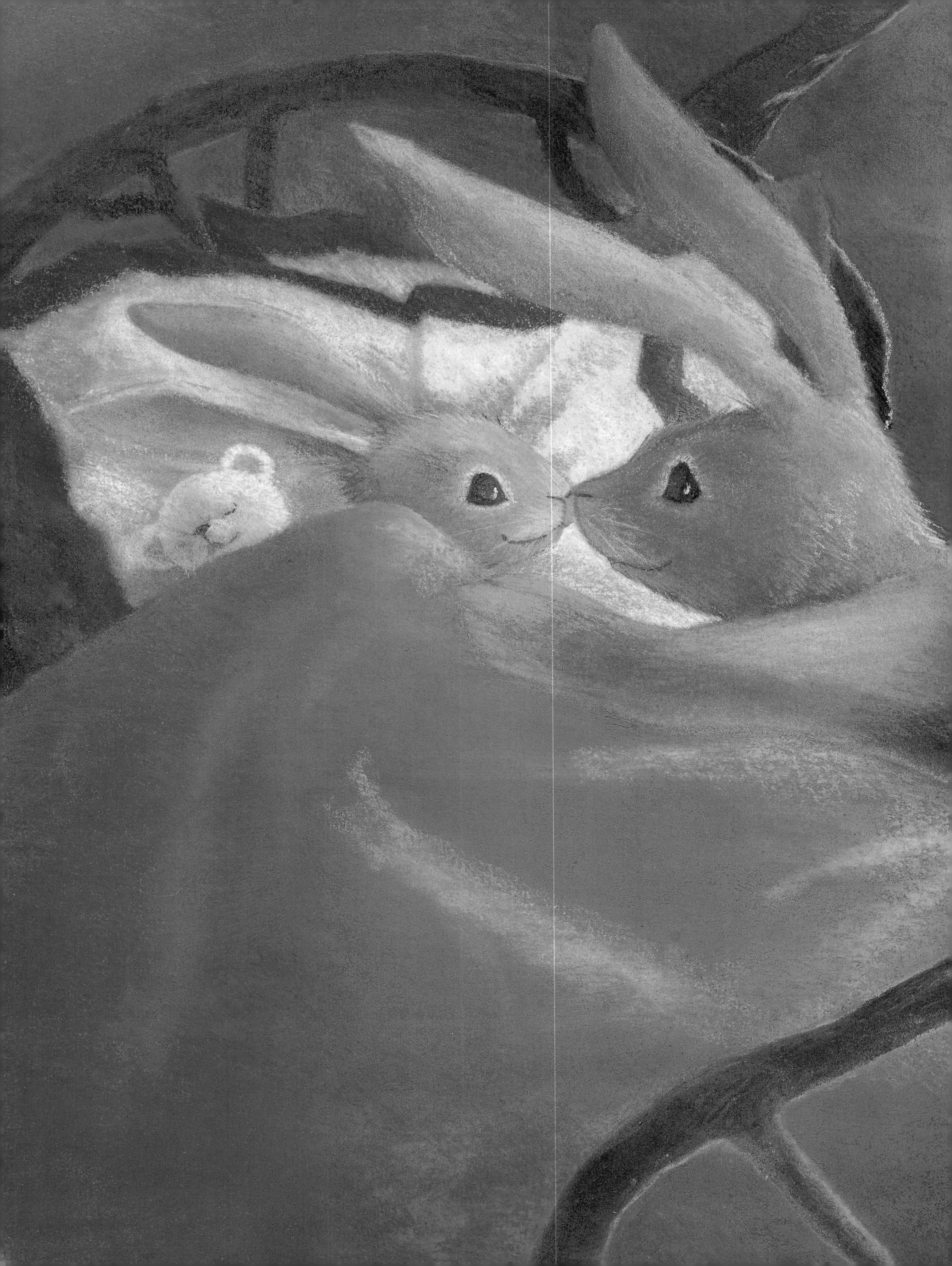

Say goodnight to the bright, pale moon,
say goodnight to the smallest stars,
say goodnight to all your toys.
Say goodnight
because just like them,
you'll be asleep and dreaming soon.

Sleep through the night
in your own soft bed.
Close your eyes,
rest your head.
Dream happy dreams.

Good night.
Sleep tight . . .

. . . till morning comes
and the sun shines bright.

Sleep tight.
Good night!”

It's Time for Bed